no man came

Books by Jaiya John

Fragrance After Rain
Freedom: Medicine Words for Your Brave Revolution
Daughter Drink This Water
Calm: Inspiration for a Possible Life
Sincerity of Sunlight: A Book of Inspiration
Fresh Peace: Daily Blossoming of the Soul
Your Caring Heart: Renewal for Helping Professionals and Systems
Clear Moon Tribe
The Day Jumoke Found His Name
Legendary: A Tribute to Those Who Honorably Serve Devalued Children
Beautiful: A Poetic Celebration of Displaced Children
Reflection Pond: Nurturing Wholeness in Displaced Children
Habanero Love: A Poem of Sacred Passion
Father to Son: Ode to Black Boys
Lyric of Silence: A Poetic Telling of the Human Soul Journey
Black Baby White Hands: A View from the Crib

NO MAN CAME

JAIYA JOHN

CAMARILLO, CALIFORNIA

No Man Came

Printed in the United States of America

Soul Water Rising
Camarillo, California
soulwater.org

Library of Congress Control Number: 2022913630
ISBN 978-0-9987802-8-3

First Soul Water Rising Edition, Hardcover: 2022

Fiction / short story

Editor: Jacqueline V. Carter

Cover and Interior Design: Jaiya John

The womb dreams. Endlessly.

- Jaiya John

Thank you for encouraging and doula-ing
me to resurrect this story, H.
I am forever grateful.

This story burst out of the womb of my soul when I was the age of 23. It was not a creative choice. It was a possession.

SOUTHERN SOIL

I came in from the cornfields muddy that day.

Girl, ya sho 'nuff gon' get da whippin' tuh yo' back side! I done tol' ya million times not tuh come in dis here house all messed up wid dirt an' such!

Mammy wadn't a big lady, wadn't but a stretch ova five foot, but she sho' could holla some. An' dat day she let out 'nuff wind an' noise tuh knock muh seven-year-ol' body right back out da do'. Only, dis day I seen sompin' in huh eyes dat caught hol' a muh heart, tugged it sompin' past frightful. She couldnuh been much pas' t'irty-five, 'cept on dis one day she looked a heap more'n dat.

I stood dere in da do'way wid da sun ridin' on muh back, lightin' up da daisies on muh dress. Dat ol' sun leapfrogged muh lil' body an' kep on over tuh Mammy. It caught huh 'round da waist an' settled dere, kinda like a skirt. Only, pieces a dat sunlight 'peared tuh climb on up Mammy's front, 'peared tuh skip on up an' 'round huh eyes. What dat sunlight showed tuh me, dough, was da face of a ol' woman.

Dis sight drew me in fo' a clos'a look, den knocked me right back from fright alone. Huh eyes 'peared tuh be goin' out, like a canduh. Like life done 'cided tuh up an' leave Mammy fo' some udder place. Da life was goin' 'way in 'em, an' blow 'em da skin sagged an' puffed, like Unca Harowd's ol' houn' dog.

Now, Mammy seen me a lookin' at huh an' she musta known what muh own eyes was declarin', big wid fright an' all, fo' she stopped hollarin' of a sudden an' huh ho' body sagged. Like a doll dat jus' got da stuffin' pult out it. She come over tuh me an' says, real sad like, *Girl, I guess ya can see right 'nuff dat da world be wearin' harder on me den it got a right tuh. Now, I don' want ya tuh be scared none, we all gotta git on in years. Just dat da Lord happen tuh bring some along faster den da rest, dat's all.*

Mammy sat down on da chaiya an' pult me up on huh lap. *Lis'en, child, I gots tuh tell ya sompin', an' I wants ya tuh lis'en good, ya hear*? She ran huh long, rough hands tru muh hair, tuggin' on da black bunches a t'ick locs. I didn't feel none too much good right 'bout den. Felt like when a to'nado come a runnin' ova da hills an' all da grown folk scurry out, all big eyed, a screamin' fo' all da children tuh come in an' take shelta.

I reckon I recall Mammy's words goin' sompin' like dis:

Now, I don' want tuh get ya t'inkin' in da wrong way 'bout certain t'ings in life, but I feels I gotta duty tuh tell ya 'bout dis here knot a pain dat been a eatin' me up fo' fah too long a spell.

I aint always been da kinda person dat ya may see me as now, girl. Back when I was a younga woman I didn't know a pot a gol' from a snake in da grass, fa' as what was right fo' me. Yo' pappy come 'round one day, all tall an' han'some as he was, an' he right swep' me off muh feet. Didn't know seed nor blossom 'bout him, didn't care tuh, jus' reckoned a body dat good lookin' an' sweet talkin' couldn't a been nothin' but good news.

Course, he was da same tear bringin', soul-breakin' devil den dat I later saw him tuh be. Jus' dat I couldn't see dat fo' nothin', muh heart was a flutterin' so. Anyhow, yo' pappy come tuh showin' his true self over da next cup'a years, an' all da time I was a fallin' deeper intuh his seductive well a' darkness.

I mighta been catchin' a glimpse a his true reflection aftuh 'round 'bout da firs' year, 'cept I was jus' a child in mind, 'fraid tuh death 'bout facin' da world widout him. Dis planted a righteous fright in da pit a muh ches', a fright dat fed like a 'coon on da scraps a muh doubts, growin' all da time intuh a monstrous beast. It ate 'way at muh strength, girl, took any independence I mighta had an' tossed it out fa' from me. I sank intuh his dark well like a hailstone racin' tuh get tuh earth.

Come a few years later, wadn't nothin' tuh muh'self da woman. I was but a skeleton on a set a strings, pult dis way an' dat fo' da pleasure of a man wid no concern but fo' his own. A man wid nothin' but hellfire burnin' in his eyes. He had managed tuh grind me down tuh dirt, an' use muh spirit as soil fo' da growth a his own demon.

Girl, in a way, I spawned da devil dat begot yo' po' soul. By da time dat he had planted yo' seed in muh belly, da world had turnt tuh an endless field a emptiness befo' muh bloody eyes. No matta how loud I scream’t, no matta how hard I prayed or how fa’ I dug intuh da earth wid muh nails, wadn't no one tuh ansa' muh call. Yo' pappy had seduced me in a world a folks an’ colorful t'ings an' such, an' dragged me tuh a place where dere was no one an’ nuffin' at all. All da colors had run away.

BLOOD THINGS

Now, by da time dees las' words come tuh muh ears, muh insides was a turnt out. Mammy's words had claws, an’ dose claws reached intuh muh ches' an' tore muh soul tuh pieces. Da devil done kilt muh Mammy, an' lef' dis skeleton here fo' me tuh lis'en tuh. I knowd long time befo' dat, Mammy wadn't all what a soul should be. But dere, in dat kitchen dat day, I come tuh know she been murder’t.

Dat was da las' time I had me a real sit down wid Mammy, until da day muh body come tuh womanhood. I woke one mornin' wid a light head, an' I 'member not feelin' right. Night befo', had me some strange feelin's in muh gut. Like sumpin' creepin' an' flutterin' down t'ward muh legs. Tol' Mammy muh dinner had gone down wrong, an' dat's what I truly b'lieved.

Anyhow, dis one mornin' I come tuh muh senses an' notice muh sheets tuh be stickin' tuh muh legs. Dem sheets was damp, too. Aftuh peelin' back da blanket, I saw dis big ol' stain a blood, spread out where I had been a layin'. Well, I hollered out a deathly scream, 'cause I was sure muh insides had come out. Right den I was 'specting tuh be sleepin' wid da soil soon 'nuff. Mammy come a runnin' in from da kitchen, flour all ova huh hands an' chest, eyes bigger'n da sky.

I was right'nuff scared, dat was plain tuh see, an' Mammy, she jus' knew what was a'happnin' from da moment she cast huh eyes 'pon muh sheets. She took tuh comfortin' me right off:

Lis'en here, child. Now don't ya be frightened 'bout what ya sees here. Dis aint nothin' but da nat'ral ordah a t'ings. Da Lord got it in his crazy mind tuh put all us womenfolk tru dis here same t'ing.

Now, ya jus' reach da point where yous a woman now, child. An' dis what happened tuh yo' body don't mean ya tuh be sick, nor diseased 'n such. It's jus' sumpin' what come 'round evuh so often, an' sho' 'nuff make ya feel bad, but ya aint gon' die from it though ya might have ya a t'ought or two 'bout dat very t'ing.

Mammy went on tuh tell me dat what dis all meant was dat I was a woman in ever' way now, an' dat meant I was fulla capable a havin' me childs now. Tol' me I had tuh protect muhself from men now, 'cause dey would soon 'nuff be wantin' tuh lay dere hands on muh body, an' how dis could put me in a bad way wid child an' all if I let dem taste muh flesh. Now, Mammy, she did talk in all kinda crazy symbols 'n such, but I understood huh fo' what huh message was meant tuh be.

Now, dere was dis one part tuh what she said dat stuck in muh mind from dat moment tuh da hereaftuh. Mammy got real solemn-like, an' creased huh fo'head, placin' huh hand on muh shouldah as she said:

I want ya tuh take dese next words an' place dem in a box in yo' head dat miss yo' heart an' reach all da way down to yo' soul. Put dem in a box what can't be broken o' fo'ced open.

Jus' as I, a woman, was da one dat come a runnin' tuh ya at dis frightnin' moment, it will always be a woman dat will come tuh yo' side, if anyone's tuh come at all. Da main worry tuh have 'bout havin' yo'self a child is dat at any time, da man dat gave ya seed tuh dat child might up an' diss'pear on ya. An' more likely den not, he up an' leave when yous needin' him most. See here, child, I done spent a lifetime witnessin' da evil a dis animal what be called man.

Ya get yo'self wid child, an' wid child is what ya come ta be: alone wid child. An' in any a' da otha times yous in need a someone tuh lean on, someone tuh keep ya afloat in dis swallowin' sea a life, it most like gonna be a woman dat does da supportin'.

An' even if a man come tuh yo' aid at a time, don' be gettin' da idea dat he gon' make a pattuhn outta it. He lift yo' hopes an' blind yo' vision, so dat ya t'ink ya got sompin' tuh fall back on when life blows ya over.

In many a way, a man dat come tuh ya once is more tuh be feared den a man what don't come 'tall.

Hear me out, girl. Yo' pappy done lef' me widout a t'ought tuh yo' po' soul. He lef' me tuh raise ya up muhself, lef' ya tuh grow up widout no pappy, widout dat presence. Dough, I do admit, I believe his presence woulda been mo' of a curse tuh ya den his absence has been.

None'da'less, when I needed one, no man came. When ya was needin' a man's love an' strength as yo' pappy, no man came. An' worship dese words, girl. By God an' Moses, worship dese words: When da time come dat yous in trouble an' desperately needin' da support an' love dat any person has a right tuh need, ya find yo'self cryin' in da dark an' screamin' at da emptiness, hearin' no echo 'cause no man came.

Now, turn yo' ear all'da way tuh me, girl. When I says da word "man," *I aint only talkin' 'bout menfolk. I'm talkin' 'bout dat spirit dat is scared tuh death a' da world an' everyt'ing in it an' believe da only way outta dat fear is tuh conquer an' control everyt'ing.*

I'm talkin' 'bout a t'ing so terrified a feelin' at all, dat it can't bear a wild t'ing tuh go free, o' determine itself. I'm talkin' 'bout a spirit a fear so desperate tuh be bowed down tuh, it will gnaw at an' contort itself intuh da most monstrous kinda t'ing.

A woman, if she get huh'self torn an' lost 'nuff, a woman, too, can be a man.

Now, I knew Mammy was full stuffed up wid pain an’ bitterness old as da bible. So I did muh best tuh suck da marrow from da bone a what she tol’. Still. Dose words done haunted me fo' da rest a muh life right on up tuh dis point.

Muh dear Mammy up an' lef' me soon aftuh dat day. Da good Lord saw fit tuh lift huh a' huh burden, ease huh pain. Da doctors said dat Mammy died of a heart 'ttack, but I knew deep in muh soul dat Mammy died cause she was robbed a' huh spirit. Aint a body dat evuh lived dat can live widout no spirit whatsoevuh. Many git by wid jus' a little spirit, but when dere aint even a drop, den its jus' a matta a time befo' da Lord come a callin'.

I'd like tuh say dat dose words muh Mammy bestowed upon me pult me along da path a' avoidance, or at least along da path a' caution, as men be concerned. Like tuh say so like nothin' I'd like tuh do.

I have a notion dat da t'ing from which ya been bred is da t'ing tuh which ya be wed. By dat I mean, da t'ing dat went on 'tween muh Mammy an' da man dat seeded me, an' da t'ing dat went on 'tween muh Mammy an' all da men she evuh encount'uhd was a force which I's inherited by default a bein' da sprout a dere soil.

Muh life aint been much worse dan a lot a people's, nor much betta dan most. Still, dere was a certain shadow dat followed me tru da course a' it, 'spite da fact dat I was 'ware tuh avoid such a haint.

SLEEPING SKY

I've got to tell you about a certain night.

It was so cold outside. The cliffside, steep and muddy. I had trouble making my way down the decline. The pitch darkness wouldn't allow me to see my feet below me. I walked on, driven by the torment of the moment, wanting it to end more even than I wanted my life to end. The strong breeze kept picking up the corners of the blanket and flapping them, as if God wanted a goodbye.

I came close to stumbling a couple of times. If I had, I would have surely kept catapulting down the hill until I crashed lifeless on the rocks. When I finally made it to flat ground, I walked out, closing in on the rhythmic tidal calls. The sand gave way as I stepped. It felt as though the weight of my crime was driving me into the ground.

I knelt down where the sand began to be moist. The saltwater from my eyes flowed freely and fell onto the sand, merging with the saltwater of the sea. As the waves lapped up near to where I knelt, I started to unfold the blanket. I noticed the tiny little bells sewn into the fabric, the way the light blue color of the blanket seemed angel-white in that night.

I stopped unfolding the blanket and wrapped it back up. Lights gleamed on the horizon of the water, small and distant ones that seemed to ebb and flow with the ocean. I screamed to the sky, but that cold sky was black and sleeping.

THE FEVER OF IT

Now, let me back up a piece.

Before that inconceivable night, I had already done a terrible thing. In the bathtub.

Later, when I told him what I had done, I saw the look in his eyes. That look utterly betrayed every word that came out of his horrible mouth. He lied because he thought the lie was what I wanted to hear, so he spat it out with the easy fluidity of smalltalk. No hesitation.

No hesitation is what he showed when he left me, too. It was a while after the bathtub, but I knew he was only waiting for appearance's sake. Until I would not see his splitting as so inhumane. So that it wouldn't seem like he was leaving because of what I had done. Right.

When this all began, weeks after the violence of his violation, and well before the bathtub, I told him that it wasn't what I wanted. That it, the consequence growing in me, should end now. It had to. I could not find words in any language to get him to grasp what I felt and knew in my soul.

I pleaded with him to help take away my burden, but he and others I dared to pour out to just preached morality and fear. They didn't know spit about my reckoning. Their souls were too dry for spit. I pleaded to God, too. God abstained.

For just a moment, I slaughtered my sovereignty.

Why, God? You bastard.

Folks went on their way. Once they thought they had tamed the wild thing, they had other priorities. And he, he left, just as I was waiting for him to. By the time he did, I was actually very relieved.

That's when I decided to do things my way.

You don't know aloneness until you are fixin' to commit what the whole world tells you is the worst of sins. In that empty remoteness, no one's love reached me at all. My own body was a cruel taunting, for it was the very ground of my betrayal. I just wanted not to have a body. I screamed my prayers, wanting only to be air and disappear from the shame and hurt of it. I would have rather floated through space forever than to face the truth stirring in my womb. The aloneness put my idea of myself in a blender, turned it on high, and walked away for good.

At first, the guilt evaporated my guts. I despised my whole soul. I found a thousand ways to lash myself. Then started over with a thousand more. Maybe you feel I had a choice. You ever had a wildfire burning in your womb? Tearing everything apart in your past and future generations? A feeling that a massive poisoned planet is growing inside the puny pebble of your body?

I kept on now, fully in the fever of it. I was decided on the unimaginable. The distance between believing that I could never do such a thing and surrendering to do such a thing was the distance of a death. I died. All my ideas of anything at all just up and died.

After destroying any belief in my own decency, I was reborn. Much of the guilt got on down the road. After all, when I wanted him to stop, he kept going. When I wanted them to stop it, they made me keep going. So I killed right and wrong. The world isn't made of those things. It's made of choices. I made mine.

I surely hadn't always taken Mammy's advice, but I sure enough was going to do right by her now. I knew if I didn't, nothing but pain and sorrow and loneliness would follow for me and for what I would bring forth from me. Sometimes your bones just know a terror beyond terror is coming. In that moment, you will do anything to prevent it. Good and bad do not mean a lick when the worst is on its way.

SO ALONE

I was home alone that red afternoon. Crows tapped on the roof. I knew they were trying to tell me something. I wasn't trying to hear them at all. I had music playing. Don't know what. I just had it on because I couldn't stand the silence. Not then.

I used an old knife from the kitchen.

The old knife had never seemed so menacing before, but as I picked it up this time, it appeared sharper and angrier than ever. It was a new thing in my hands. An awful memory being born.

The bathtub was cold. So were my tears. I never knew tears could be so cold. I brought the phone into the bathroom because I knew I would be in danger. I also had a lot of towels. And a pot of hot water for no reason at all that I can fathom now. I sat an old stuffed rabbit from when I was a girl up on the edge of the tub. I closed the small window above the tub, not wanting to traumatize my neighbors. I remember a red dragonfly outside beating against the glass. I kept the light off.

An hour or so earlier, I watered the plants in my bedroom and swallowed maybe half a bottle of pain tablets. I fought and gagged hard against the reflex to throw up. I can't remember most of that day, that moment, or the moments after. What I am telling you now is the horrible leftovers of it.

I sat there in the tub. For just a second I allowed myself to hope that maybe just one man would come and save me, come and save us.

I snuffed out that moment in disgust. I spit at the image of him, thrusting savagely over me, caring not about the sensations I was feeling, much less about my pleas for him to stop. I fantasized. I killed him with a bullet of my rage in that instant. Then I prayed to God, and cursed God, too.

Then I began.

The old knife was even colder now.

It spoke all the syllables of cruelty as it violated my flesh.

I lay in the pool of blood, screaming. I had thrown the knife against the mirror above the sink, shattering it. I hurt more from the thought of my insides and what they cradled being shredded than I did from the actual physical pain. But, dear Mammy, it did hurt so bad.

I had already made the phone call. I screamed at the person on the other end, like she was the one who had done this to me. I screamed all of hell at that poor woman and then I screamed some more. Tasted blood in my throat. Still do.

For what seemed like an entire day, I lay there, blood coming still, the music from the other room laughing at me. I laughed back, maniacal with a sick, despairing violence and hate.

For the length of what felt like an endless dream, I kept drifting in and out of consciousness. My head was feeling more and more light and dizzy. I knew I was going to die.

As I started to black out completely, Mammy's face appeared in my mind. It started to mouth something. I couldn't quite make out the words. Even so, the sound of her ran right on through me. Her voice took me back to a memory.

Mammy used to braid my hair out on the creaky porch in the sunrise light. Her twisted hands glistened with butter as she gathered my strands. Her touch on my scalp felt like her love, only without her old pain mixed in. Sometimes, I heard her softly humming, like she had a butterfly of joy in her mouth that she couldn't set free. She would catch herself and fall back into silence.

Mammy was so uncomfortable loving me softly and openly, meaning she was shy about showing me her remnants of joy. I was content to let her bury her poor heart in worryful scoldings and naggings. I hoped her love for me could still grow, even without the touch of sun.

Only after Mammy's face appeared as I was blacking out did they come. I was taken to the hospital and the men in white there saved my life...

So that I could suffer some more.

People I knew came by those next few days to see me. I was pitied, scolded. Empathized, sympathized, cried with. I received many bright flowers, stuffed animals, books, and cards. No one offered me silence. You know, sit with me in silence and let the moment be enough. What I had just gone through, it isn't a thing to philosophize about. Life just feels to me like a giant merry-go-round of losing things. If you lose too many things, folks will get to avoiding you. Or telling you what to do.

None of those cold, empty hospital offerings mattered, of course. Despite almost killing myself, I had failed. I still had not stopped it. It was still growing. I felt the cells divide inside me.

Those days spent in the hospital were good for me. I was allowed the time to reason through the terrain of my life. By the morning I was to leave, all was reconciled within my mind.

I had to visit the waters as soon as it was out of my body and in my arms.

STARLESS SKY

I'm so sorry, dear child of mine. My own foolishness helped to conceive you. Your angel heart should never have beaten in the light of this world. I tried to save you from it before you could see the light, but I needed help. No man came.

I tried to do it my way because they wouldn't do the same for me. They could have done it right and your precious soul would now be resting peaceful up there in the darkness.

See that up there where the stars don't shine? They're hiding because they're ashamed. But soon you'll be with them. Warm. Bundled and safe.

No. They couldn't, wouldn't help me do it, so I tried it alone. Even then I hoped for them to come, but only for a piece of time. No man came.

Oh, God, where are they now?

Just this once, will someone come?

No.

I must put you to sleep now, my child. Drift gently on the waves, drift out there and beyond. Drift to where my Mammy is. I Love you.

I left the faded blue blanket on the beach.

It probably blew into the ocean.

I fought myself that night. I clawed and scratched at fate, at the powers above, at the evil below. I begged and wailed. I pounded the sand and kicked the waters. I tore out my hair, and screamed so long and hard that blood flew from my mouth. I held her so tight, so tight. In the end, for the last time until eternity, I swear, I waited by the waters... but no man came.

I loosened my grip on my baby and let
her die in the ocean.

Oh, Mammy, ya sho' nuff woulda been proud a’ me.

I washed da sand off muh feets befo' I went back home.

If this story touched you, you can truly touch it back.

Please kindly consider writing an **online reader review** at various booksellers. Reviews are a valuable way to support the life of a book and especially an independent author.

Freely **post social media photos and videos** of the book and you reading from it. Please kindly include the hashtag **#jaiyajohn.**

I deeply cherish your support of my books and our Soul Water Rising rehumanizing mission around the world.

BOOK ANGEL PROJECT

Your book purchases support our global *Book Angel Project,* which provides grants and books for vulnerable youth, and places gift copies of my *medicine books* in communities worldwide, to be discovered by the souls who need them. These books are left where hearts are tender: hospitals, shelters, nursing homes, prisons, wellness centers, group homes, mental health clinics, and other vital community spaces.

If you are fortunate to discover one of our *Book Angel* gift books, please kindly post a photo of the book on Instagram, using the hashtag **#jaiyajohn**, or email us at **books@soulwater.org**. Thank you much!

I Will Read for You:
The Voice and Writings of Jaiya John

A podcast. Voice medicine to soothe your soul, from poet, author, and spoken word artist Jaiya John. Bedtime bliss. Morning meditation. Daytime peace. Comfort. Calm. Soul food. Come, gather around the fire. Let me read for you. **Spotify. Apple. Wherever podcasts roam.**

Jaiya John was orphan-born on Ancient Puebloan lands in the high desert of New Mexico, and is an internationally recognized freedom worker, author, and poet. Jaiya is the founder of Soul Water Rising, a global *rehumanizing* mission to eradicate oppression that has donated thousands of Jaiya's books in support of social healing, and offers grants to displaced and vulnerable youth. He is the author of numerous books, including *Fragrance After Rain*, *Daughter Drink This Water*, and *Freedom: Medicine Words for your Brave Revolution*. Jaiya writes, narrates, and produces the podcast, *I Will Read for You: The Voice and Writings of Jaiya John,* and is the founder of *Freedom Project*, a global initiative reviving traditional ancestral gathering and storytelling practices to fertilize social healing and liberation. He is a former professor of social psychology at Howard University, a former National Science Foundation fellow, and holds doctorate and masters degrees in social psychology from the University of California, Santa Cruz, with a study and research focus on intergroup and race relations. As an undergraduate student, he attended Lewis & Clark College in Portland, Oregon, and lived in Kathmandu, Nepal, where he studied Tibetan Holistic Medicine through independent research with Tibetan doctors and trekked to the base camp of Mt. Everest. His Indigenous soul dreams of frybread, sweetgrass, bamboo in the breeze, and turtle lakes whose poetry is peace.

Learn more at: JAIYAJOHN.COM

Jacqueline V. Carter again served graciously, faithfully, and skillfully as editor for *No Man Came*. I am forever grateful for her Love labor.

Secure a Jaiya John keynote, talk, or reading:

jaiyajohn.com

OTHER BOOKS BY JAIYA JOHN

Jaiya John titles are available online where books are sold. To learn more about this and other books by Jaiya, to order discounted bulk quantities, or to learn about Soul Water Rising's global freedom work, please visit us at:

jaiyajohn.com

books@soulwater.org

@jaiyajohn (IG FB TW YT)

JOURNAL YOUR SOUL HERE.

JOURNAL YOUR SOUL HERE.

JOURNAL YOUR SOUL HERE.

CPSIA information can be obtained
at www.ICGtesting.com
Printed in the USA
LVHW111641130822
725885LV00003B/55